Lazy Mary

A read-together book

Lazy Mary

Lazy Mary, will you get up, will you, will you, will you get up

Lazy Mary, will you get up, will you get up to-day.

Story based on a traditional song by *June Melser*.
Illustrations by *Judy Shanahan*.

Programme designed, edited and graded by *June Melser*.

ISBN 0-86867-048-0

First published 1980. Reprinted 1981, 1982, 1982, 1983, 1984, 1984, 1985, 1986, 1987

Published by Shortland Publications Limited, 360 Dominion Road, Mt Eden, Auckland, New Zealand, and Rigby Education (a unit of RPLA Pty Limited), Melbourne, Sydney, Brisbane, Adelaide, Perth, Australia.
Distributed in the United States of America by The Wright Group, 10949 Technology Place, San Diego, California 92127, U.S.A.
Distributed in Canada by Ginn & Company, 3771 Victoria Park Avenue, Scarborough, Ontario M1W 2P9, Canada.
Published in Great Britain as "Story Chest" by Arnold Wheaton (the Educational publishing division of Pergamon Press), Parkside Lane, Dewsbury Road, Leeds, LS11 5TD.
Distributed in Singapore and Brunei by Federal Publications (S) Pte Ltd, No. 2 Jurong Port Road, Singapore 2261.
Distributed in Peninsula and East Malaysia by Federal Publications SDN BHD, 8238 Jalan 222, Petaling Jaya, Selangor, Kuala Lumpur.
Printed by Colorcraft, Hong Kong.

Lazy Mary

Lazy Mary,
    will you get up,
Will you, will you,
    will you get up?

Lazy Mary,
    will you get up,
Will you get up
    today?

What will you give me
for my breakfast?

A big, big egg.

No, Mother,
    I won't get up,
I won't, I won't,
    I won't get up.

No, Mother,
    I won't get up,
I won't get up
    today.

Lazy Mary,
    will you get up,
Will you, will you,
    will you get up?

Lazy Mary,
    will you get up,
Will you get up
    today?

What will you give me
for my lunch?

A big, big pie.

No, Mother,
   I won't get up,
I won't, I won't,
   I won't get up.

No, Mother,
   I won't get up,
I won't get up
   today.

Lazy Mary,
    will you get up,
Will you, will you,
    will you get up?

Lazy Mary,
    will you get up,
Will you get up
    today?

What will you give me if I get up?

A splash
of cold water
if you don't!

Yes, Mother,
    I will get up,
I will, I will,
    I will get up.

Yes, Mother,
I will get up,
I will get up,
today.